# MOOKI
## THE BERRY BANDIT

Written by
### Kari Smalley Gibson *with* Gary Smalley
Illustrated by Barbara Spurll

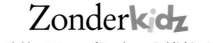

Zonder**kidz**

*The Children's Group of ZondervanPublishingHouse*

*Mooki the Berry Bandit*
Text copyright © 2001 by Kari Smalley Gibson
Illustrations copyright © 2001 by  Barbara Spurll
Requests for information should be addressed to:

**Zonderkidz**™

*The Children's Group of* ZondervanPublishingHouse
Grand Rapids, Michigan 49530
www.zonderkidz.com

Zonderkidz is a trademark of The Zondervan Corporation.

ISBN  0-310-70100-7

*Edited by Gwen Ellis*
*Art Direction by Jody Langley*
*Design by Tobias Design | Outerwear for Books*

*Printed in Singapore*

01 02 03 04 / 5 4 3 2 1

# Dedicated to...

### Roger,
My best friend, my spiritual motivator...the most wonderful
husband and daddy in the world. You have my heart forever.

### Michael,
You love life to the fullest, dream the biggest dreams, love with all
your heart. You are the joy of my life!

### Hannah,
My mighty miracle, my adorable cuddle bug...the sunshine that
brightens my day. All my dreams came true when you were born.

A special thanks to my Mom, Mimi, Erin, Denise, JuJu, LaLa,
Patty, and Donna. Dear friends are the best "Happies!"

Thank you Angela Ellett and her classroom of amazing kids...
you all are angels!

## Illustrator's Dedication

### To Don

It was fall festival time in the big forest. Mooki and all the other forest critters always looked forward to rides and food and games. This year they were especially excited because there was going to be a new ride—the BuzzSaw Coaster Ride. Whoever won the grand prize for the bake-off would get to ride it absolutely *free*.

"I must find the juiciest, the most spectacular berries in the whole woods if I'm going to win the Harvest Festival bake-off contest!" Mooki Beaver said even though no one was listening.

He plucked an itty-bitty wild strawberry and squinted at it. *This is way too ordinary for my pie*, he thought. *And besides, it would take a million of them to get enough for one pie.* Mooki had been searching all day long for some perfect berries for his prize-winning pie. He made up his mind that he would win no matter what he had to do.

*But how am I going to win if I can't even find decent berries to put in the pie?* He walked over to a small garden behind his house. A crooked sign hung from the shiny red gate. It said, "DO NOT TREZPAS." Hmmmm, thought Mooki. *This is the blackberry patch where my friend Gibby the bear is always working.*

Peering around cautiously to make sure no one saw him, Mooki opened the gate. *Creeeak!* The noise was loud in the quiet forest. He slipped in quickly and pulled the gate shut. *Creeeaaak!* It was even louder this time.

"Wowsy, look at all these berries!" Mooki said right out loud. "I wonder why some are black and some are red? Oh well!" And he plopped right down on the ground and started picking as fast as he could. Mooki's berries went *Plop! Plop! Plop!* as they hit the bottom of the bucket. He looked over his shoulder every few minutes to make sure no one saw him in Gibby's garden. He picked so fast he didn't even take time to pop a single berry into his mouth. As soon as his pail was full, he stood up and slipped out through the gate. *Creeeak! Creeeak!* He scurried down the path toward his house.

A s soon as Mooki got home, he gathered everything he needed to make his yummy pie. He washed the berries and stirred in sugar and spices.

Mrs. Twizzer, a very wise opossum lady, came into the kitchen. "My you're busy, Mooki. Oh, by the way, did you see anyone in Gibby's berry patch today?" she asked. "Someone stole all his berries."

Then Mooki did something very bad. He lied. "No, Mrs. Twizzer, I didn't. Maybe whoever took them *really* needed them."

"No, Mooki," said Mrs. Twizzer. "It is never right to take something without getting permission first…even if we think we *really* need it."

Mooki didn't say anything, but he started to feel sick inside. Quietly, he poured the berries into his piecrust and put on the top crust. Then he put the pie in the oven to bake.

When his pie was finished, Mooki set it on the windowsill to cool. Then he went to see what the others were doing. Gibby was as busy as could be.

"Hey Mooki, how does my shortcake look?" asked Gibby proudly. "I can't believe I didn't burn it."

Mooki shrugged his shoulders and mumbled. "It looks okay." Truthfully, Mooki was amazed. Gibby had baked an enormous shortcake and covered it with lots and lots of tiny strawberries. Then he had topped it all off with wild mint and gooey honey sauce. It looked *fabulous*.

"I keep dreaming of soaring through the air on the BuzzSaw Ride," Gibby said. "Do you think I have a chance to win?"

Mooki mumbled miserably, "Mmmm Hmmmm."

The next day the kitchen buzzed with excitement. Mrs. Twizzer wrapped loaves of lovely warm bread. The whole place was full of baked treats. It smelled heavenly!

"*Squaaaawk! Oh no!*" Payton the Peacock was squawking his head off. "My cake sank in the middle! HELP!" All the critters giggled and giggled. "I know what I'll do." Payton cocked his head, and his little crown tilted. "I'll do *this!*" He plopped a huge flower right in the middle of the sunken cake. It looked pretty good.

Meanwhile, Mooki thought, *I have to make this pie look extra special if I'm going to win.* So he plopped whipped cream all over the top. Getting ready for the contest should have been so much fun, but Mooki wasn't having fun. He was miserable, and he knew why. The stealing and the lying were making him sick inside.

"All right everybody. It's time to head to the Harvest Fair. Gather up your goodies and follow me," shouted Mrs. Twizzer.

As they scurried to keep up with her, everyone chattered about the ride on the BuzzSaw. How fast would it go? How scary would it be to ride? And who do you suppose will get to ride free?

"Look!" yelled Gibby. "There it is!"

They all scrambled over to the huge contraption. Mooki couldn't believe his eyes. It was the biggest coaster ride he had ever seen. His hands began to tremble with anticipation, and looking down at his glorious pie, he thought, *I just have to win the bake-off. Then maybe this awful feeling will go away.*

The Harvest Fair was buzzing with activity. Delicious smells drifted out of the brightly colored tents. People in booths were selling honey corn and candied apples. There were baskets full of acorn cookies and berry tarts in every corner. There were jugs of hot clover cider.

"Whee!" laughed Gibby. "I have to taste everything!"

Mrs. Twizzer smiled, "First, all of you who entered the bake-off must take your baked goods to that large, yellow tent for judging."

Mooki was eager to get rid of his pie. So he went quickly to the judging tent and handed it to the first judge he saw.

"Your pie looks lovely," declared Hannah the hedgehog.

Mooki smiled a weak little smile. He just wanted to get out of there as quickly as possible. Maybe then, he could run away from the awful feeling inside.

*This is the worst day of my life*, thought Mooki. *I wish I hadn't stolen Gibby's berries.*

Mrs. Twizzer noticed the expression on Mooki's face and walked over to him. "What's wrong, Mooki? You look like you just lost your best friend. Do you want to talk about it?"

Mooki shook his head slowly. "No, Mrs. Twizzer. Th…There's nothing wrong," he whispered. "I just don't feel very good." He wished he could tell Mrs. Twizzer the whole story. She might be able to help him. But then Mooki decided he was just too ashamed to confess that he had stolen Gibby's pretty red and black berries.

"It's okay," she said, giving him a hug and scuttling off to help the judges.

Each of the three judges took a big bite of the first treat. First, they checked to see if it looked good. Then they checked to see if it tasted good. Sometimes they went back for one more bite to see if it was *very* good.

Oh my, they were having a splendid time tasting all the goodies. *"Yummy!"* … *"Sticky and gooey!"* … *"Mmmm!"* … *"Tasty!"* they said as they smacked their lips. Finally, they got to the last two entries—Gibby's wild strawberry shortcake and Mooki's black and red berry pie.

A huge grin spread across Gibby's face when the judges took big bites of his shortcake. "Umm hum!" they said and nodded their heads.

*Oh, why didn't I pick those boring little strawberries instead of stealing Gibby's berries?* thought Mooki. *Why didn't I tell Mrs. Twizzer the truth?* Then all the judges picked up Mooki's pie, opened their mouths, and each took a huge bite. Mooki covered his face with his paws. "It's going to be just fine, Mooki." Mrs. Twizzer put her arm around him. "Your pie is very pretty. You don't need to be afraid."

What happened next looked like an explosion!

"*Auuuugg!*" shrieked the first judge as he spit the pie back onto the plate.

"*Icky!*" choked the second judge while still trying to swallow his bite.

"*What in the world…!*" yelped the third judge, using his napkin to try to wipe the berry taste out of his mouth.

The judges rushed to the clover-cider jug, almost colliding as they darted across the tent.

"What's going on here?" demanded Mrs. Twizzer. "What's wrong with Mooki's pie?"

"It's bitter."…"It's terrible."…"He used berries that weren't ripe!" The judges spewed out the words along with red berry juice.

Mooki was humiliated. He charged out of the tent and burst into tears.

Mrs. Twizzer came out too and was the first one to reach him. She put her arms around him. "Mooki, it's all right.  You didn't know."

"It's not all right!" sobbed Mooki. "I stole Gibby's berries because I wanted to win the contest soooo much."

"Oh Mooki." Mrs. Twizzer stepped back and looked at him.  She was very concerned as she knelt down beside Mooki. "Stealing is never right.  You knew that and that is why you are feeling so miserable.  I am so sorry you chose to do the wrong thing. You hurt yourself a lot, didn't you?"

Mooki nodded his head and looked into her golden eyes.

"And those awful feelings grow bigger and bigger until finally you feel you're going to burst with guilt.  What's even worse is that when your friend, Gibby, finds out what you did, he will be hurt too."

Mooki  couldn't look up.  He was so sorry for what he had done.

"There is a way to wipe away those terrible feelings." Mrs. Twizzer smiled. "First you need to ask God to forgive you. Then you need to tell Gibby the whole story and ask him to forgive you too," Mrs. Twizzer told him. "Gibby is going to wonder what happened to his berries when he takes a look at his berry patch. So what do you say we talk to God first and ask him to forgive you. Then you can go tell Gibby and ask for his forgiveness."

After they had prayed, Mooki stood up and looked around for the furry bear.  There he was. Oooo, this was so hard.

"Gibby, I did something really wrong, and I need to talk to you about it." Mooki began.

Gibby looked surprised, and he sat down next to his friend.

"I took your berries," confessed Mooki shamefully. "I wanted  the biggest, best berries in the woods so that I could win the contest, and your berries were just jumbo! So I took them.  I know what I did was wrong. I'm sorry, Gibby. Will you forgive me?" asked Mooki tearfully.

"Gibby grabbed his buddy and gave him a huge big bear hug. "Sure, I'll forgive you," he said. And they walked off with their arms around each other's shoulders.

Mooki asked, "Mrs. Twizzer, why did my blackberry pie taste so sour. Those red and black berries were so big and juicy when I picked them. I…"

"You picked red blackberries?" Mrs. Twizzer asked. "Blackberries are only ready to be picked if they are completely black. "Red blackberries are not ripe."

"Wowsy!" replied Mooki with a grin. "No wonder they were so awful."